Critical acclaim for Peter McGehee's *Beyond Happiness*

"The light comic touch, keen sense of the absurd, and conversational style that leaven McGehee's later work are evident already in these breezy tales about growing up 'different' in an uptight Arkansas family. Billy's suspect sexuality is among the book's central concerns, but the real focus is on his dysfunctional Little Rock clan: a wilful mother, a destitute father, and assorted crazy aunts."
— *Quill & Quire*

"How witty, unsentimental, and sharply detailed McGehee's writing is …"
— *The Village Voice*

"McGehee is always observing, always tracking idiosyncrasies, always searching for the fresh way of seeing and reporting."
— *San Francisco Chronicle*

"What an imagination!"
— *The Body Politic*

"Scented with gardenia and just a hint of diesel exhaust."
— *Bay Area Reporter*

Critical acclaim for Peter McGehee's *The I. Q. Zoo*

"*The I. Q. Zoo*, a new collection of his short stories, shows ever more clearly that McGehee's talent was as a comic miniaturist…. These stories are remarkable for a minimum of description and introspection. Still, since they are set amid the ongoing tragedy of AIDS, they do not lack a sense of gay rage, feelings of impotence and a hefty dose of survival humor."
— *Lambda Book Report*

"McGehee [in *The I. Q. Zoo*] writes more about characters 'on the edge,' and sometimes, unbalanced by the weight of living itself, going over that edge."
— *University of Toronto Quarterly*

"[*The I. Q. Zoo*] shows McGehee extending his range and emerging as a writer of talent and individual style."
— *The Toronto Star*

"The 12 short stories that are collected in *The I.Q. Zoo* provide a second glimpse of McGehee's power and versatility as a storyteller….The short story format is particularly suited to McGehee's talents – especially his ear for dialogue and use of humorous anecdotes. Thematically, the journey into the nature of love he leads us on in *The I. Q. Zoo* is not dissimilar to the one we take in *Boys Like Us*; it is the variety of styles, narrative techniques, and types of characterization McGehee makes use of that make these stories so striking."
— *Paragraph*

"Peter McGehee writes witty and gritty tales, often from the wild side of gay experience. He's a writer with no innocence at all, only an unblinking acceptance of diverse behaviours.
— *Books in Canada*

"McGehee has a wonderful way with a wacky, Southern-Gothic-in-the-blender shaggy dog tale; 'The I.Q. Zoo' is a terrific saga of death and a two-bit roadside zoo."
— *Quill & Quire*

Critical acclaim for Peter McGehee's recent novel *Boys Like Us*

"Peter McGehee has a deceptively light touch. *Boys Like Us* pulls us into a world we recognize instantly and travel through effortlessly. The surprise is how well McGehee uses the ordinary details of our daily lives to evoke the demons we all struggle with: sex and love, friendship and family, life and death. I look forward to his next book."
— Helen Eisenbach, author of *Loonglow*

"An utterly delightful book. I enjoyed every word of it!" — Quentin Crisp

"… an upbeat, quirky, often humorous and ultimately optimistic book filled with snappy dialogue and colorful eccentrics."   — *The Toronto Star*

"The novel takes a mordant, unsentimental view of the AIDS epidemic…. a sex-positive novel, a rarity in this age. We are definately not in Jesse Helms' territory."   — *The New York Times Book Review*

[*Boys Like Us*] is full of the raffish, down-homey, surrealistic humor that [Zero's] birth clan in Arkansas and his adoptive family of gay men, mostly involved in one form of show biz or another, both use to maintain their equilibrium against the slings and arrows of each other's, as well as fortune's outrageousness. A genuinely delightful comedy so full of tangy dialogue and wacky situations that it screams for the stage, or better yet, the screen."   — *Booklist*

"… a slice of life so deftly spun that there is no question of putting it down …. hilarious good comic writing."   — *The Vancouver Province*

"… an effortless and consistently entertaining read…. We need more novels of urban manners this funny. We need more laughter that resonates against the serious issues of our lives."   — *Quill & Quire*

"McGehee has the ability, through an invigorating style and witty observations, to transform Zero's everyday life into something we care about. McGehee's intelligence shows through on every page."
— *The Boston Guide*

"…a pleasant, often humorous novel, with fun and imaginative character…. the two chapters in Arkansas could be right out of *Steel Magnolias*."   — *Library Journal*

"Irresistible – a playful romp through contemporary gay life."   — *Xtra*

BEYOND HAPPINESS

The Intimate Memoirs of Billy Lee Belle

PETER McGEHEE

Copyright 1983 and 1985 by Peter McGehee. Copyright 1993 by the estate of Peter McGehee.

Second edition.

99 98 97 96 95 94   5 4 3 2 1

All rights reserved. No part of this book covered by the copyrights hereon may be reproduced or used in any form or by any means – graphic, electronic, or mechanical – without the prior written permission of the publisher. Any request for photocopying, recording, taping, or information storage and retrieval systems of any part of this book shall be directed in writing to CanCopy, 214 King Street West, Suite 312, Toronto, Ontario M5H 3S6.

All characters and events depicted in *Beyond Happiness* are fictitious. Any resemblance to persons, living or dead, is strictly coincidental.

Cover illustration and design by Dik Campbell.
Book design and typesetting by Val Jakubowski.
Author photograph by Doug Wilson.
Printed and bound in Canada.

Parts of *Beyond Happiness* have appeared in *Pink Ink* and *Rites* in slightly different form.

Beyond Happiness has been produced as an evening of theatre and performed by the author. Its first performance was July 2, 1983 at the Jazz Club Theatre in Saskatoon, Saskatchewan. A central Canadian tour, including Toronto and Montreal, followed. The show ran Off Off Broadway beginning February, 1984 as a part of the "Theatre Night at Fold City" Series. Subsequent engagements included the Jim Diaz Gallery in New York and the Valencia Rose in San Francisco.

The publisher gratefully acknowledges the financial assistance of the Saskatchewan Arts Board and the Canada Council.

Canadian Cataloguing in Publication Data

McGehee, Peter, 1955-1991

  Beyond happiness

  Originally published: Toronto : Stubblejumper Press, 1985.
  ISBN 1-55050-050-3

  I. Title.

PS8575.G435B49 1993   C813'.54   C93-098028-X
PR9199.3.M443E49 1993

COTEAU BOOKS
410 - 2206 Dewdney Ave.
Regina, Saskatchwan
S4R 1H3 Canada

For
Douglas Wilson
and
my parents

CONTENTS

PART ONE
What Is Happiness?	3
My Short Career as a Female Impersonator	9
A Poodle in the Pool	13
Run Out of Little Rock	17
A Housewife at Last	25
Just Another Waitress	29

PART TWO
The Day I Met My True Love	37
My Mother's Divorce	43
I Took My True Love South	47
White Woman Turns Black	53
Beyond Happiness	57

PART ONE

What Is Happiness?

MY MOTHER'S BIGGEST FEAR WAS THAT I'D TURN OUT GAY. Her second biggest fear was that I'd write a book about it. Her third biggest fear was that I'd write about her, which is exactly what I ended up doing.

Mother Dear has lived a life plagued by misery. No twist of fate, nor thrust of Dame Chance has ever been seen by her as having any positive value, oh no, just one more menacing inconvenience to bear. Naturally, she wanted for her children what she had failed to find, in short, happiness. She made it her special mission to do everything within her power to eradicate any obstacles she might perceive to stand in the way of that goal. These included sex, aside from the missionary position which was beautiful, communism, and the wonderful world of entertainment.

As a young child stuck in the South, I found these concepts quite alarming. I was bright enough to realize I was out of step with the world around me but I didn't care, that's just the way I was. I hated sports; I liked playing with my little sister's dolls. I hated fighting; I liked a good, clean discussion. I hated being disappointed by "real" people, so spent the majority of my time in my imagination. Needless to say, Mother Dear grew increasingly concerned.

My very first visit to the psychiatrist was based on just this account. I was six years old and hadn't a clue why I was being hauled to such a doctor. Feeling physically fine, I inquired what it was I might be sick with.

"It's a different kind of sickness," I was told. "It has to do with paying attention in school."

True, Forest Park Elementary bored me beyond belief, but I had maintained an above average score. The need for medical help in this department remained a point of confusion.

"Never mind," my mother assured me as we lurched off in her large, over air-conditioned car. "You ought to be making straight As. I know I did."

■

The doctor was a thin man of middle age. He wore a dark suit and had lots of books on display. He asked me to close my eyes and feel a series of objects, telling him what they were: coins, pencils, a letter opener. In no time at all the visit was complete.

That night the episode found its way into my sexual fantasies. I dreamt of a handsome, young doctor who asked me to shut my eyes and feel his coins, his pencils, his—

On the way home I asked my mother more insistently, "What was that all about?"

"I am just seeing after your happiness, dear."

"But I'm happy."

"No you're not. You just think you are."

"Then what is happiness?"
Obviously my mother knew, but she wasn't going to tell.

■

The following Thanksgiving I witnessed a scene at a family dinner concerning my Aunt Suzy Knocks that began to give me a few clues.

Suzy was my favorite relative. When visiting her you could do whatever you liked and eat what you wanted. All rules were suspended for the madness of the moment, madness being one of Suzy's strongest suits.

Suzy married into our family. She was never liked by the adults, and because she wasn't really "one of us," open venom directed to her was excusable. She and my Uncle Patrick rarely participated in family events due to this tension, and when they did, she invariably drank too much.

Suzy was forty-five, weighed ninety pounds, and had no eyebrows. She had plucked them out during high school and they had never grown back, so each morning she drew them on to suit her mood. That day they were thick, black, angular bars. She was anticipating the presence of my Great Aunt Tula.

Tula Scull was, is, and will always be an enormous woman. Thanks to the timely deaths and disabilities of her three sisters, she is the ruling matriarch of the family. She does exactly as she wishes, has rarely been crossed, and answers to no one.

Aunt Tula's full of outrageous opinions and plenty of contradictions. I remember once seeing her at dawn, thundering out of her bedroom, stuffed into an old pair of Levi's, carrying an arm load of fishing gear, and cursing her awkwardness. A few hours later she was immaculately dressed, seated at the head of the lunch table, and carving a large catfish with a big, shiny knife.

Suzy came from a family that didn't hold the tradition of an undisputed ruler. She thought Tula overbearing, pompous, and a bore. Tula, in turn, was worse than anybody about Suzy. She had no patience, compassion, or sense of humor concerning carefree alcoholics.

Patrick had been the one to insist on having everyone at the same table for dinner. He still hoped someday his beloved bride would gain acceptance.

Cocktails were abundant. There was little talk of pilgrims and none of God. There was a lot of talk about how long a turkey ought to cook and whether there were enough oysters in the oyster casserole. Tula said she was certain her hostess was in no shape to manage culinary duties and it wouldn't surprise her in the least if the whole thing came out underdone. Why this was even an issue was beyond me. Suzy's dinner, like all of my aunts' affairs, would be cooked and served by a black maid.

After another series of slightly disguised condescensions, Suzy, not sure how much longer she could hold her tongue, exited to the kitchen. She mounted a stool and engaged in several large martinis, solitaire.

The table was a lush setting for sixteen. Patrick put Tula at the head and Suzy at the tail. By this time Suzy was very drunk. She didn't touch her food. While the rest of us gabbed and ate our way through the enormous feast, she just watched us with a curious contempt, sipping her wine.

As Aunt Tula reached for the second turkey leg, Suzy finally spoke. "Tula Scull, you are the fattest damn woman I have ever laid eyes on in my life!" Suzy stood up, turned on her heels, and staggered off in the direction of the living room.

There was a loud crash. Patrick rose with the impulse to see what had happened. Tula stopped him with a slight motion of her hand. A self-satisfied smile upon her lips, she nodded and again lifted her fork. Dinner would continue in peace. Suzy would be left wherever she might have landed.

I couldn't wait to finish so I could go check on her. When I did, I found her face down in an African violet, sprawled halfway on and halfway off the coffee table.

She'd been crying. She looked at me, then began to finger her pearls. "I've been wanting to say that to that bitch for the last twenty-three years."

As I was helping her upstairs I told her I was sorry.

"Sorry? Don't be sorry for me. Regardless of what you may think, I am a very happy woman. It's them you ought to be sorry for. They haven't got any idea."

She went into her bedroom and shut the door. I stood in the hallway speechless. Some instinct inside of me knew what Aunt Suzy had said was true. All doubt was gone from my mind.

The next day, in excited confidence, I went to my mother and told her, "I've finally figured out what happiness is."

"What?"

"Aunt Suzy!" I announced with pride.

■

The following week I was again taken to see that psychiatrist, only this time my confusion had turned into something a little more concrete.

As I sat there answering the doctor's questions, I began to resent Mother Dear tremendously. I knew that happiness lay far beyond her obsessive concerns, and I intended to find out where.

My Short Career as a Female Impersonator

WHEN I WAS NINE YEARS OLD, MY FATHER TOOK ME TO SEE *The Sound of Music* starring Julie Andrews. I was heavily influenced by the epic nature and sense of comraderie I witnessed upon the screen. It was almost as good as *The Wizard of Oz*, which I never missed each year when it was shown on TV.

I couldn't let another year go by without putting on my own theatrical extravaganza. I longed to taste stardom.

Much to my luck, the school talent show was in the process of being cast. Late one day after school, I walked up to that time-slotted sheet and signed on as "opening act." I thought I, if any, could fulfill the challenge.

The script would be a combination of all my favorite stories. I would star as the heroine, Dorothy von Andrews.

Our teacher, Miss Horton, was to direct. "There won't be any rehearsals," she informed us. "I'm trusting each of you to work up your parts on your own. We'll put the show together on opening night. We'll perform it in the style of an ancient pageant."

Miss Horton was a horror story unto herself. She predated the Acropolis, wore Chinese silk dresses, and great amounts of powder and cheap perfume.

The evening of the performance I left home on a speeding bicycle. I carried a suitcase full of costumes and props. I used the Safety Patrol Office, one of my favorite spots, as a changing room.

I cannot begin to describe the thrill that tingled throughout my body as the curtain went up on my scene. I was stretched out on an imitation chaise longue looking not unlike Cleopatra. I had on a red dress, belted at the waist, and black, patent leather, high-heeled shoes. My hair was a simple terrycloth bath towel pulled back into a fashionable ponytail. Above my eyes I had drawn thick, black, angular bars. I wore my mother's heirloom pearls and held a champagne glass thrust grandly into the air.

Before I could get out the first line of "There's No Place Like Home," a great and hideous wall of laughter engulfed me from the audience. I said a swift prayer of thanks that my parents were out of town on business. I didn't lose all hope of recapturing the drama until I looked off into the wings and saw Miss Horton laughing hardest of all.

I felt so nauseous the only thing I could think to do was run to the boys' washroom, but Miss Horton stopped me. She said, "Get back out there. You were hysterical! Finish your scene."

I tried to warn her of my illness, but she wouldn't listen, not until I vomited all over the front of her elegant gown.

A few days later she phoned my mother to see if she was prepared to pay the expensive dry cleaning bill. She must have told her the whole story because after they hung up, Mother Dear came into my room. I was in bed reading a book on baseball as penance. She was confused and angry, and said through clenched teeth, "Tell me you're not a homosexual! For God's sake, tell me you're not!"

"Of course not!" I snapped. I knew I couldn't tell her the truth. Though I was only nine, had the right man come along I would have gladly given him my hand in marriage.

Tension grew at school. Fighting was a big sport and there wasn't a boy who didn't challenge me. I always refused, knowing I hadn't the proper training to win. Soon, a polite decline was not enough. I began finding an ever growing gang of them waiting for me by my bicycle after school. It was only by use of clever talk that I managed to undo my lock and race away. Finally, it was arranged with Miss Horton that I leave five minutes prior to the bell in order to get a safe head start. I was soon a complete prisoner to my pacifistic nature.

My mother suggested cattily that I engage in a boxing class at the "Y," an idea I dismissed immediately.

"But hadn't you better learn how to defend yourself like a man?"

"No."

"Then don't think you can come crying to me."

"I wouldn't dream of it."

I ran away. I didn't get far, just two blocks.

When I went back up the steps that led to our house, I swore never to waste my talents on an ungrateful audience again. I realized for the time being my career as a child star must play second string to my surviving grade school. I longed for the day I would leave Little Rock, for the much warmer and more welcoming world of strangers.

A Poodle in the Pool

NATURALLY DEATH, UNLIKE LIFE, IS WHAT OCCASIONALLY afforded me episodes of freedom. Uncle Patrick, who had suffered from heart problems since his early thirties, decided to die suddenly while at a convention in Hawaii. Aunt Suzy decided he would be buried in Houston. The Arkansas branch of the family herded into station wagons. Off we went to offer condolences.

The best part about such pilgrimages was that I was usually separated from the rest of my family. I was beginning to be perceived as a young man, and a young man needs to slowly be delegated responsibility.

Uncle Patrick's mother, Aunt Killy, was in the hospital with problems all her own. Her cherished companion, an irritable poodle named Trina, was in Aunt Suzy's care.

Trina was just this side of sainthood. No beauty treatment, special diet, or privilege was too extreme. When home with Killy she dined on deviled crabmeat and was taken for twilight drives. When kept by Suzy she was treated like the neurotic bitch she was.

In light of the grievous circumstances, the responsibility of watching and feeding Trina was transferred onto me. Gladly, I accepted. There wasn't any place I would have rather stayed than with Aunt Suzy.

Trina, as always, was impossible. She refused to eat, bit you if you tried to pet her, and stayed up half the night pacing the kitchen floor, her little painted nails going click, click, click, click, click.

The only time she was halfway human was when she stood by the sliding glass doors that led out to the patio, pool, and garden. For it was there, beneath the azalea bushes, that she was permitted to do her business.

Responsibility has never been one of my fortes. Trina tripled the challenge. She was thirteen years old. I had known her all my life. I was very fond of dogs in general but had a definite problem with particular poodles.

The night before my uncle's funeral she was clicking to beat the band. Aunt Suzy hadn't slept in three days. The dog had to be stopped.

I considered giving Trina a tranquilizer but knew I'd never get her to take it. I boiled some hot chocolate, which I knew she loved, and laced it with several ounces of kahlua.

My scheme worked. She sat on the edge of the couch through the entire run of *What Ever Happened to Baby Jane?* I was into the kahlua also. Happiness was indeed ours.

The next thing I knew, I awoke with the remote control in my hand, the television all fuzzy, and Trina scratching to get out. Groggily, I went to the door, opened it, she ran out and peed, I shut it, and went back to bed.

At eight o'clock the next morning my sweet dreams were cut to the quick when I heard Aunt Suzy scream in horror out on the patio. I rushed out to see what she had seen and when I saw, screamed too. Guilt and shame flooded me as I witnessed a sight too terrible to be true – Trina's corpse floating around the pool.

How had it happened? Hadn't I let her back inside? And even if I hadn't, could she have possibly been so drunk as to fall in the swimming pool and drown on her way to the azalea bushes?

Aunt Suzy instructed me to go to the garage and get the cleaning net. We tried fishing her out, but to no avail. Eventually, I had to swim in and try to haul her up by hand, but every time I'd get close enough to grab her she just seemed to sink further down. When I finally managed to get a hold of her rhinestone collar and began to pull her to the side, one of her hind legs got stuck in the drain and twisted terribly out of shape. Then on dry land what were we to do with her? She was bloated to twice her normal size and as stiff as could be. She wouldn't fit in the garbage can. We had to call a vet and pay for a cremation service.

I tried to apologize, but Aunt Suzy wouldn't hear of it. "Trina should have been put out of her misery years ago. I don't know why they leave her with me anyway. I've always hated dogs. So did Patrick."

She grew teary-eyed and suggested we have breakfast. We also had a bottle of champagne. "Patrick would have wanted us to."

Aunt Suzy told me she was glad I was there, that she wasn't particularly happy to see the rest of the bunch, but that I was different.

I sat with her in her dressing room while she put on her makeup, drew on her eyebrows, and did up her hair. I felt so sad. I knew with Uncle Patrick gone we wouldn't be seeing much of Suzy anymore.

When the hearse arrived to pick us up, she took my arm and bravely smiled. "This isn't going to be an easy day."

■

The funeral was completely upstaged by the Trina tragedy. Even the preacher was more concerned with how Killy would take the news rather than my uncle's soul speeding to Heaven.

It was decided Killy be told Trina had a coronary. All present swore never to tell the truth. The tale remained intact for years to come.

The next day, when we were driving back to Little Rock, I felt homesick, but didn't know what for. I was stuck in the back seat, pressed against a window. I thought about Suzy, about Trina, and about life.

Funny how the humdrum goes on forever and the good parts so quickly blur, just like scenery in the distance.

Run Out of Little Rock

IN MY LAST YEAR OF HIGH SCHOOL I WAS TO EXPERIENCE divine love and I don't mean through Jesus Christ. Bruce Cocklin and I had been best friends for the better part of a year. We shared our innermost thoughts, embraced on occasion, and cried together unashamedly at sentimental movies.

Initially, we took our affection to be that of just "friends." I don't know how much paper we wasted writing one another quotes from *Jonathan Livingston Seagull* and Kahlil Gibran. You may well laugh at our naiveté, but did we care? Not on your life.

Most weekends were spent double-dating. Bruce would take Rowa Lou Barton; I would take her best friend. I loved Bruce, but certainly not in a way homosexual. Still strangely, he excited me: his slender body, friendly smile, and curly brown hair. When with him I forgot all about my troublesome family and existed in a state of pure delight.

Perhaps my feelings were just fashionably "bi," but I wasn't about to lose the best friend I'd ever had by suggesting we engage in experimental sex.

Our friendship remained as such until the following winter. In early January I had to go to Dallas to audition for the Theatre Department at SMU. Though my parents trusted me with the car, they felt someone really ought to be with me for the five-hour drive. Bruce was the logical candidate and his parents were more than happy to let him go.

It was pre-arranged with a home town boy that he would put us up in the dorm. He did so, but in two separate rooms. My heart yearned, longed, and lusted for experience, but that night, like so many of my youth, was completely forgettable.

The next day my audition went well. I was accepted into the department, though they had serious qualms about my Arkansas twang. I was so thrilled, I sang my own version of "I'm the Greatest Star" skipping thorough the freshman quad, Bruce by my side.

"Damn," I said. "Here we are miles from home and stuck in a stupid dorm."

"I was thinking the same thing."

"We ought to do something crazy."

"Like what?"

"I don't know, but if we were staying in the same room at least we could stay up all night."

"Why don't we go somewhere else?"

"Like where?"

"Dallas must be full of cheap hotels."

I smiled real big. "What a perfect idea."

We drove around until we spotted a white, stucco, "Greekesque" motor inn. It was slightly disheveled, but looked relatively clean. We went in and asked an overweight, indifferent clerk the price for a room.

"Ten dollars for one bed, twelve-fifty for two."

Always economical, we decided we could only afford the ten dollar room. As I was signing the register, he asked me if it was for the afternoon or would we be staying all night? I thought that an odd question. "Why, the night, of course." I took the key. Room twelve. The Roma Motel.

I remember the layout of that room to this day: the mermaid art, the vinyl chairs, the soiled carpet. It was paradise.

That evening I offered to take Bruce to dinner. My father had slipped me a credit card. We settled on one of those chic little steak places with a railway car theme. We ate, drank, talked, gazed, and lingered. It was total intoxication, yet not once did either of us feel the least bit drunk.

My next memory is being back at the Roma. We were stretched out on the bed, our heads at the foot, chins on crossed arms, vaguely watching TV.

Jim Nabors and Julie Andrews were on some special together and she looked so strange. She had on this black, sequined body-suit. Her hair was tinted an odd, menacing shade of grey.

The room was warm. We were in just our underwear. White, cotton jockey shorts.

When the show ended, one of us reached up and turned off the set. We talked a bit, dreamy and tired, then decided it was time for bed.

"You gonna get the light?" I asked.

"No, you."

"You," I insisted. I was excited and didn't want to get up and walk across the room. Then I saw he was in the same state.

"It happens," he said.

"Yes it does."
"Did I ever tell you you were gorgeous?"
"Knock it off."

As we got into bed, his foot brushed against mine. His feet and hands have a particular touch of softness that I will never forget.

We said goodnight, each unaware that we would soon take that long awaited dive into wonderous and forbidden love.

We embraced as we always did, only this time we didn't let go. We lay with our heads on either edge of the same pillow looking into one another's eyes. Slowly we began to touch. Bravely outlining each other's face, neck, shoulders. When I kissed him he was tentative at first, so I just rested my lips against his, the sweetness of boys' breath interchanged.

We were tender as we tangled, every inch over and over again. We discarded our silly underwear and were lost to the night as one. Outside the neon sign flashed through the blinds across our bed reading, "Roma, Roma, Roma." When we awoke, we repeated our love. There was no past, no future, just Billy and Bruce.

■

The next day when we got back to Little Rock, I was so depressed I could have died. By making clever use of a Carole King song, I managed to tell Bruce how I felt. I found out he felt the same way. What we had started, we had no choice but to continue.

The months that followed were absolute bliss. We managed to spend at least one night a week together. We'd go out on our usual double dates with Rowa Lou and her friend, take them home early, then go to my place or his.

For both of us, it was our first experience with sexuality. We were incorrigible. Often we'd say we had to study together after school so we could lock ourselves in my room and recreate our fever. We auditioned for community theatre so we could attend the same rehearsals. We wrote love notes which we exchanged in the hallway at school. Sometimes we even met in the boys' washroom simply to tease one another's pleasure. I was in a constant state of breathlessness.

Unfortunately, it was only a matter of months, until like a couple of careless criminals, we were found out. Bruce's mother was putting her son's clean socks away into his dresser. Beneath the underwear, she noticed some notes. She didn't hesitate to have a read. She was touched at first, naturally assuming they had been penned by Rowa Lou. When she saw my signature, she fainted cold, hitting her head on the bedpost as she went down.

When they found her they rushed her to the emergency room. She suffered a nervous breakdown, then in conference with her doctor, began to explain why.

We denied everything, saying the knock she had received must have left her deranged. She was still in possession of my notes though, and there, in my very own handwriting, was our incrimination.

She threatened Bruce severely. Her doctor assured her it was me who was homosexual. Her son had just been lured into my sticky, immoral web.

The weeks that followed were awful. It was hell to try and meet, much less do anything but brood when we managed to. I just couldn't understand how such pure feelings of love could be so successfully destroyed by the evil interpretation of somebody else. How much I had to learn.

We considered running away, but figured we'd end up hating one another. That was the last thing we wanted.

Soon fate took all decision out of our hands. It was only a matter of time until Mother Dear heard and where else would she hear but at Adrienne's House of Beauty? She rushed straight home, puffy from crying and reeking of hair spray.

"What kind of pervert are you? If you're afflicted with a bizarre kind of puppy love, we'll take you to some doctor and get you fixed!"

I stared at her. Her look of frenzy and panic made me speechless. I knew I had to get away, and get away fast.

I secured a job at the farthest, most remote corner of the state. I was to be a cave guide and spend the summer underground with middle class tourists. It seemed somehow perversely poetic, something, thank God, I would eventually outgrow the need for.

As I boarded that Greyhound bus to begin life on my own, a long, bitter taste turned into a strange, unexpected glee. But as I looked back at the platform, at Bruce waving sadly goodbye, my heart went dark. I ached for him.

We wrote crazed letters of love all summer long. They began to dwindle off in the fall. At Christmas he told me he had decided to go straight. Within a year, he was married to a girl from his college at Shreveport. I felt terribly betrayed at first, as though the world had ended. I hated him and I hated myself.

In time I came to understand. They were quite upfront with one another. She was going to support them and he was going to raise the kids.

■

They've been married ten years now. I still see Bruce on occasion. When I pass through town we sometimes meet for drinks.

And no matter how much time goes by, when he looks in my eyes that feeling is still there. Billy and Bruce.

A Housewife at Last

AFTER THREE YEARS OF BEING A GOOD, SERIOUS THEATRE student, method acting and method life began to lose its appeal. It wasn't at all what I'd had in mind creatively speaking, and a change was necessary.

I longed to travel, but that was a bit impractical, since I had no money. It was also the beginning of the term. I did the next best thing I could think of. I turned to drugs and had my first experience with LSD.

I denied its effects vehemently at the time, but it had a dramatic impact upon my life. A great amount of my fears were suddenly abolished. My ingrained work ethic seemed absolutely absurd. I broke through an amount of conditioning that would have taken me years in the more conventional setting of therapy. Zen Buddhism came to me like a flash of pure light.

My parents began to worry about me more than ever. One night in a spasm of going with the flow, I drove all the way to Little Rock to announce that I loved them. They were horrified.

I had one semester of school left and was on full scholarship. I began toying with the idea of really letting go, deserting the contents of my apartment, and taking that quantum leap into life itself.

What I really wanted to take a leap into was full-time love. There had been no one in my life like Bruce Cocklin for three years. I was ready and willing to give it my all.

During spring break, a small group of us soothed our wanderlust with a trip to San Francisco. While there, we attended the Patty Hearst trial. I've never been quite sure why, perhaps her SLA/Tania drama delighted our stupidity, but it was in that courtroom that I spied the handsome, sexy, and well-traveled Steve Stephens. Bells rang once again.

Our eyes met over the throngs of spectators. It was only a matter of hours until we were walking up and down Ocean Beach, arm in arm. We spent three days together. They were eternity. Each of us confessed that real love, for which we had always searched, had at last been found.

Back in Texas, all I could think of was Steve. His bed, his city, his cafés, his gorgeous California. He'd write me letters calling me magical and wise. He'd been a conscientious objector to the Vietnam War and had taught school in Tizi Ouzu, Algeria. He had even lived in Europe!

I longed to surrender my better senses, and this time there were no parents, there was no nosy Mrs. Cocklin poking around the underwear drawer looking for tell-tale notes. Besides, no one I knew even wore underwear anymore.

Four weeks prior to graduation I did exactly as I had envisioned; I quit school and left. My parents gave up all hope that I settle down and become normal. They pleaded any concession if I would just finish my degree.

"Nonsense!" I announced. "I've got the knowledge, who needs a silly piece of paper that says I do?"

Wasn't it ironic that in the mid Seventies, I would dive head first into the racy and radical Sixties?

Steve and I rarely worked. We didn't want to contribute to the capitalist system, we just wanted to be supported by it in a minimalist style. We collected unemployment and food stamps. We went to the beach five times a week. We meditated. We discussed reincarnation. We visited eccentrics, of which Steve knew plenty. My head was full of a newness and wonder always longed for, but seldom met. It was my Renaissance. I even became a vegetarian.

By the end of the summer we reached our goal of renting a farm house on a small acreage in northern California. There we would grow our own food and wait for the inevitable end of the world. At last, I was a housewife.

To my dismay, within a week of being there, Steve decided he no longer wished us to be lovers. He said it was no longer real to him.

In a panic, I found myself out on a limb of a tree whose name I didn't even know. I thought of my buddies back in Dallas. They'd be moving to New York soon to become the stars of tomorrow. What a fool I'd been. I had wanted to be completely cut off and that is exactly what I'd received. I stared at walls like an idiot. My emotions were an inexperienced roller coaster of uncertainty. The only thing that made any sense was to get a dog, which I soon did.

As it turned out, the passion between Steve and me continued, but on his terms and what a trap that was! I thought I could successfully transcend, but I couldn't, nor could I leave. I thought somehow things would again be as they once had. Like Penelope of ancient lore, I would sit and wait.

Six months later Dame Fate, the one thing I have always been able to count on, mailed us an eviction notice. For lack of better ideas, I struck out on a seven month hitchhiking trip with my dog and a baldheaded actress from L.A.

My "divorce" from Steve continued to be a source of disillusionment. Every month or so we'd talk on the phone, each lonely and wondering if we shouldn't give it another try.

At the end of my journey I returned to San Francisco. Two days after my arrival Steve was offered a job with an American school in London. He would leave for England the following week.

Freshly devastated, I rented a room on Haight Street.

Over the next several years my addiction to him still seemed impossible to break. We often took holidays together. The contrast of our incompatible dispositions, yet ridiculous desire for a relationship retarded any and all attempts to be free.

Slowly but surely, this housewife became a feminist, the feminist soon a separatist, and inside that separatist lurked an embryonic gay man who childishly wanted it all.

It was time for me to forget my preoccupations with romance and Prince Charming. It was time for me to implement a process of elimination and find out what really was important.

One day I found myself standing in the middle of the gay ghetto waiting for a bus at Eighteenth and Castro Streets. I was staring at a wall of graffiti on the side of the old Star Pharmacy, but I only saw one word. "Community." Why had it taken me so long to realize I wasn't alone?

Just Another Waitress

WHEN ALL ELSE FAILS, IT'S NEVER TOO LATE FOR A COMEBACK in the theatre. San Francisco seemed a likely enough place to accomplish such a goal, but when I set out to do so I was confronted with a cynical, if not completely indifferent market. It soon became painfully apparent I would have to supplement my income with work in the restaurant business.

I secured a position at a place in the financial district appropriately called Mr. Toad's. The job lasted ten days. I dropped and broke three dozen crystal flower holders.

It took more than a few years, and a few restaurants, before I actually developed the art of retaining a job. By then so much of my time was occupied with part-time work, political awareness, and occasional dating, that my career in show business was once again cast upon the back burner. Though this saddened me, I really didn't know what to do about it.

I had a lot of acquaintances and spent a good deal of my time at the Café Flore trying to figure out what made all of them so full of self-importance and me feel like such a nobody. I quickly came to prefer the "political tables" to the "artistic" ones due to this fact, and I found their conversations intriguing.

I longed to do something great, but couldn't think what. Sexual politics, leftist law, grassroots organizing against the bomb, what, pray tell, was the significance behind such jabber? I tried, on the condescending advice of a couple of cappucino drinkers, to read Marx, Neitzsche, and Mao. Though I was very much in favor of socialism, the death of God, and Chinese smocks, I had great difficulties with their publications. I normally read newspapers for their entertainment sections alone. These periodicals didn't even mention such bourgeois luxury. I needed to start simply and at my own back door.

I heard that a new newspaper was starting up in the gay community and I volunteered to do an article for them. My first assignment was to interview two women from the Parents of Gays Association, something I didn't even know existed.

The interviews were full of touching anecdotes. I was completely charmed by the women I talked to. How unlike Mother Dear they were: supportive, up on the issues, and willing to fight for social change. During our last session, one of them asked me if I had told my parents I was gay.

"Well, no. They'd never speak to me again if I did. Besides, they know, it's just something we don't discuss."

"Do they speak to you much now?"

"The usual. Christmas, my birthday."

"Could your relationship be much worse?"

"I never thought of it like that."

"Well, imagine for a moment if every gay person were to tell their families, if every parent, cousin, aunt, and uncle had to deal with it. Society would change. It would simply have to because there wouldn't be anyone left untouched."

That evening I wrote a short note home confirming my mother's life-long suspicions to be true. Within a week, I received a reply. How close they felt to me thanks to my brave honesty. They wanted me to come visit, suggested we have a week at the lake. They even sent a plane ticket. I went, wide-eyed.

I arrived July seventeenth, the hottest day of the year. That familiar humidity greeted its lost son with the enthusiasm of a dead gardenia. My parents had moved into a tiny condominium as my father's business luck had jinxed. He was working for an insurance company for a third of the salary he had grown used to. My mother had learned to hate him. She hated his lost drive and she hated his indifference to losing it. She'd even been secretly toying with the idea of divorce, but felt their combined debts would mean financial bankruptcy, which was then out of the question.

While at the lake, we all did our best to pretend that none of this was going on. My mother even conceded it was fine for me to be gay, so long as I didn't talk about it, never brought a lover home, and, "Isn't it about time you got a real job?" My father said it was none of his business.

I quickly came to realize that the visit had not been arranged on account of me. It was Mother Dear's last attempt to pull us all together before we finally fell apart. It was a desperately manipulated memorial.

I spent most evenings in the porch swing with my little sister, swatting mosquitoes and talking. She said she thought our parents had gone completely crazy, that they rarely exchanged a civil word, and hadn't shared a room for several years.

I asked her why she still lived with them.

"Because it's cheap."

On my last night, I went into the kitchen and found my mother crying over the dishes. I asked her what was wrong. She said, "I am just as miserable as I can be and I don't see any way that's ever gonna change for me. That doesn't make it very easy to get up in the morning. I'd just as soon be dead."

She asked if she could speak to me confidentially and told me she was having an affair, what did I think about that? I said I thought that was good for her.

"But you've got no morals."

"Well, life isn't black and white, is it? The rules don't necessarily work, not even for you."

"I'm almost ready to believe that. Look at you. You haven't got a thing to call your own, yet you seem happier than any of us. Why?"

"I don't know. Maybe it's because I'm doing what I should be."

She rolled her eyes as only Mother Dear can do. "There's something else I want to tell you. It's about your father. He has a 'thing.'"

"What do you mean a 'thing?'"

"A funny thing he likes to do. He's had it since before we were married. He told me about it even then and I accepted it. I even participated in the little fantasy, but not anymore. He's grown careless since he's had all this job trouble. Last spring your sister walked in on him. She probably never would have noticed anything had I not made such a scene, but I cannot have that. I just cannot."

My father, it seemed, took pleasure in emulating my

mother. He simply liked to dress up.

"That's nothing to be so concerned about," I said. "Even Ann Landers will tell you that."

"I am not Ann Landers, am I? Lately I've felt certain it has to have something to do with the way you are today. Why do you think I took you to see that psychiatrist when you were six years old? I was so scared, even then, when you wouldn't play ball like all the other boys."

The missing link to my childhood suddenly fell into place. The source of her great fear for my masculinity had something to do with her guilt over playing a willing part in my father's little ritual. It seemed so petty. So petty, and so small.

I had come home and faced my mother with a truth. A circle was now complete. Whether she knew it or not, she had very little power over me.

As I stood there looking at her, I asked myself what was left? What was there beyond the blown up and distorted figure my mind had made her into all these years?

What I saw before me was a very sad woman, from a strict place, in a disillusioned time. She had been bred for a world that no longer existed, if it ever did. Odd, a reality that included the Great Depression and the Second World War had no place for real life and consequential feelings. No, they were to happen in the shadows where what was expected could not be disturbed.

She was more alone in her grief than anyone I had ever known. It was difficult to let myself see her as pitiful as she seemed. I closed my eyes and held her as she cried.

PART TWO

The Day I Met My True Love

THE ONLY GIRLFRIEND I EVER HAD DURING HIGH SCHOOL was the short, shy, and chubby, Nancy Wackersly. Nancy was a star student in my mother's journalism class and our dating had been arranged by Mother Dear. Though we went steady for four months, we were never any more sensual than the occasional kiss. This was largely my doing, because to kiss, under the circumstances, seemed more than enough.

Nancy was an expert on the organ. She had a part-time job playing for rosaries at her neighborhood funeral home. I'd often accompany her, these being our more memorable outings.

On one side of a curtain would be the coffin, corpse, and mourning family; on the other side, the organ, so we could whisper and make faces without being heard or seen.

Nancy usually played Bach. I often dared her to break into something like "Hello Dolly," but she was never quite the good-time-gal I was prepared to be. In fact, the only time I remember seeing her crack a single smile was prior to the service when the undertaker would admit us to warm up the organ.

I'd go straight to the coffin, prop up the corpse, rearrange its position, and maybe even pop a cigarette in its mouth. Once I almost got her fired when I put a baseball cap on an old lady. I forgot to remove it before the service began. When the mourning family Hail-Maryed by and saw their deceased loved one sporting a little red cap that said, "The Arkansas Traveler," they laughed hysterically. They couldn't calm down. The service had to be restarted three times.

When Nancy and I decided to call it quits, I thought that would be the end of her presence in my life. Wrong. I might have been prepared to let her go, but Mother Dear was not. For years to come, anytime I was anywhere near Little Rock or Nancy happened to be anywhere near a place I might be living, she was painfully paraded out in hope that the mere sight of her would be enough to straighten me up.

During the last year in which I was living in San Francisco, three of Nancy's brothers lived there, too. They were enrolled in the Catholic University. She was to visit them in June. I learned of her plans when Mother Dear called and said Nancy would be phoning. "And you had better be nice. If not for her sake, then for mine."

When Nancy called, I used my good sense and decided to throw a brunch. My roommate, Tom Quinlan, had a friend visiting from out of town also, from Saskatoon, Saskatchewan. I was familiar with Saskatoon because I knew it was the home town of that forlorn visionary, Joni Mitchell. Though I'd never met Tom's friend, I insisted he be invited to the brunch also. The more the merrier.

A week prior to the engagement, my life fell apart for the hundredth time. I was despondent and decided the best thing to do was go away for a few days and collect myself. I settled on Yosemite National Park. I would hike into the wilderness and isolate myself among nature.

When I got there, I was so terrified of being eaten by a grizzly bear that I spent my entire time on the edge of a very popular campground watching tourists rough it in Winnebagos.

I needed to leave San Francisco. I was in a definite rut. I needed to stop sitting around cafés and I needed to write more plays. But most of all, I needed to stop thinking about love. Why did I let that quest rule my every waking moment? I promised myself I'd change.

Back in the city the morning of the brunch, and feeling a great deal better about myself, I was whipping pancake batter like a wild thing. We lived on the crest of a hill. At the appointed hour I looked out the window, and sure enough, there came Nancy, huffin' and puffin' toward our building.

When I heard the doorbell, I donned my most welcoming smile. But when I thrust it open, it did not reveal a winded Arkansan. Far from it! There stood a blue-eyed, blond Canadian. His smile was radiant. I felt immediately weak. "Well, you look a live one!"

"I am," he assured me and walked past to greet Tom.

"Dennis!" Tom exclaimed, embracing him. "How great you look!"

Didn't he though? I watched them disappear into Tom's room, then heard Nancy's familiar voice, "Hi!" She had an accent just like Gomer Pyle. She wore bermuda shorts and her legs were white. She inspected my humble home with a critical eye. She told me all about her job as a city editor with the *Houston Post* and her rather large paycheck. At any minute, I expected her to propose.

I flipped pancakes feeling more and more depressed. Just when I was going to give up on love, someone like Dennis would have to come walking through my front door.

When the four of us sat down to brunch, I found out he had a paying job working for an association that defended the rights of the wronged. He'd come to the city to march in the Gay Freedom Day Parade.

I guess it was rude of me, but I didn't pay much attention to Nancy. I just kept talking to Dennis. Finally, she said she had to go and told me I was a wonderful cook.

A few minutes later, Tom got up to make a phone call, leaving the two of us alone. Though I'm usually quite shy in situations like that, his smile made me brave. I forgot all about my vows and said, "What are you doing tonight?"

"Nothing much, why?"

"Maybe we could meet down at the Café Flore for a cup of coffee or something."

"I'd love to. What time?"

"Ten."

There was a pause.

We looked down at our plates, neither anxious to leave the table. Then I said, "Maybe we ought to meet sooner, like this afternoon?"

"Around four?"

"Four would be perfect."

There was another pause.

I smiled and said, "What are you doing now?"

"I've got to find some poles for the banner we're supposed to carry in the parade tomorrow."

"Poles? We've got poles down in our basement. Come on, I'll show you."

We descended three flights. Once through the threshold, we embraced madly. After we confirmed the existence of poles, we went back upstairs and immediately to bed. We fit like a glove.

We met again that evening and were together constantly for the rest of his stay. We wrote letters frequently after he left, often three times a day, and we phoned every other night. A month and a half later, we met in Vancouver. In the fall, I visited him on the prairies.

■

A few years passed by before I saw Nancy Wackersly again. I was in Little Rock. She came at me from across the shopping mall. "Why, Billy Lee Belle! What are you doing with yourself these days?"

"Oh hi, Nancy, lots. I've been living up in Canada the last few years."

"Canada? How'd you end up there?"

"Do you remember that morning you came to brunch?"

"I sure remember those pancakes."

"Do you remember that guy from Canada who was visiting my roommate?"

"Oh," she said, losing her enthusiasm.

"We've been together ever since."

"Well, in that case, I better get over to Sears 'fore they close, pick up my new microwave. Be sure and tell your Momma hello. Bye, Billy Lee. Bye."

My Mother's Divorce

I WAS IN THE MIDDLE OF WRITING A SONG WHEN I GOT definite word about my mother's divorce. The telephone rang and the conversation began as always. "Well," she said. "You're still alive!"

"Hello, Mother Dear."

"What are you doing?"

"I'm working on a musical."

"Really? What's it called?"

"*Big Dyke Goes West.*"

"Billy Lee, don't you know nobody wants to see a musical about a bunch of lezbeeanns?"

"Really? Did you call to harass me, or have you got something to say?"

"I called to tell you that tonight your father chased me out of the house with your granddaddy's saber. Jerked it right out of its decorational frame and all, and I'm not going back. In case you're interested, I'm staying with Aunt Clo.

Your father's lost another job. I don't know who's gonna take care of him but it certainly won't be me. If you had any sense, you'd do your duty by us and come home. But then again, you don't care. We're just family."

"I do too."

"You do not."

"Yes, I do."

"No, you don't. You just want to get all the details so you can write more stories about us. Nobody appreciates the way you parade our private lives all over the printed page! Besides, divorce is not simplistic. We're almost bankrupt. Somebody has got to see to the business matters. We have to keep the legal fees to a minimum."

"Then, why don't you call Freddie or June? They're within a couple of hundred miles, I'm thousands away."

"I did. Your brother is in the middle of Gestalt Therapy, whatever that is. He claims he hates us all. And your sister is an emotional wreck. She can't hardly take care of herself, much less anybody else."

"Isn't it interesting that in times of extreme stress, I am the only one in any shape to cope?"

"That is because you ignore us the rest of the time."

"I'll be there over Christmas. That's in six weeks and the best I can do."

"Fine." She hung up with a bang in my ear.

■

Mother Dear, the previous fall, had been appointed to an executive position with a textbook company. Her salary was higher than anything my father had ever seen. They had agreed, during sessions with a counselor, when their condominium sold to use the money against their debts,

MY MOTHER'S DIVORCE

then move into separate apartments.

My father didn't really believe the Southern Belle he'd worked and bled for his entire adult life would quite soon leave him penniless, jobless, and without a car, or a place to live. She did though, and he went temporarily insane.

When I arrived, I met with both their lawyers to help tie up mutual business. I had become my parents' parent. I didn't like the role. I thought it might make me feel of use, but all my efforts had little effect. Sadly, I realized there wasn't anything anyone could do.

Christmas Day I was stuck at my mother's apartment with a copy of the *National Enquirer* and my dear Dennis miles away. At two-thirty, I emerged into a gray and chilly afternoon to go meet my father. He had a present for me, the only one he was giving that year.

We rendezvoused at a bus stop across from his local McDonald's. He looked old and bewildered sitting there, and so, I think, did I.

He handed me an envelope. I smiled and opened it. Inside I found a membership to the SMU Alumni Association. My bankrupt father had spent three hundred dollars on something I'd never wanted and would never, ever use. I did a lousy job of covering my disillusionment. I just said, "Why, Dad, why?"

"Because it'll mean something to you in later years."

"Later years? What?"

"A newsletter, discount tickets to your football games, something you can count on."

"How many times have you known me to go to a football game? You could have used the money to pay your rent."

"I'm sorry, son. I just wanted to do something for you."

I couldn't believe the bleak emptiness in my gut. Does misunderstanding keep beating down upon us until we're so depleted we'll surrender on any terms? How I hate Christmas.

We both stood up, realizing we had nothing left to say. We headed off in opposite directions.

Halfway down the block, I turned around. My father had turned around, too. He held up his hand. I held up mine.

■

A few months down the line, he secured a job as a gardener at the Governor's mansion. Within a year, he made a good marriage to a widow with a sprawling, five bedroom bungalow.

Mother Dear discovered sex, and an abundance of eligible married men. Though she'd never admit it, she seemed quite content to be fifty and free.

I Took My True Love South

IT WAS ONLY A MATTER OF TIME UNTIL I TOOK DENNIS TO the South. He'd never been, nor had he met any of my family. Of course, it was impossible to convince Mother Dear we were coming for any reason besides throwing our lifestyle in her face.

"We want to see the real you," she pleaded, "not some fantasy!"

The real me was captured in a painting that hung in her living room. In it, I was three years old, dressed in a white suit, and completely dependent upon her.

My brother, Freddie, took a similar attitude. He phoned a week prior to our departure to inform me we weren't welcome in his home as he wasn't prepared to explain homosexuality to his three year old son.

I asked him, "What's to explain?"

"Don't be defensive," he said.

"Fine. I'll see you in the next life."

Our first evening was dinner at my mother's. She decided to meet our plane. My Aunt Lorna came with her in an effort to keep her calm.

As we walked down the ramp, she took one look at me and scowled. "You would have to come dressed like a clown!" Off she trotted.

I had on red tennis shoes, white pants, a T-shirt, and suspenders.

When we got to the parking lot it became clear Mother Dear and Lorna had come in separate cars. I was ushered into my mother's tank. Dennis would accompany my aunt.

"Well," I said, "you certainly engineered that with your usual finesse."

"Billy Lee, I might remind you this is Little Rock, not San Francisco. You cannot expect people to accept him like your wife."

"I'm not asking people to accept him like my wife."

"Oh, aren't you?"

"I told you when I planned this visit it wasn't one particularly for your benefit. If you can't be civil you simply won't see me."

"I think it's rather unfair for you to resort to threats."

"I'm sorry you make me do it."

■

Dinner was a fiasco beyond my wildest dreams. It all began when Mother Dear accused me, "The only reason you're here is for a free meal and a place to sleep."

"That's right. That's exactly why I just traveled three thousand miles."

"You ought to be slapped into the middle of next week."

"I dare you."

After she slapped me, she grabbed a good handful of my hair and began yanking it as though she intended to pull it right out of my scalp. The scuffle was so intense, we tripped over a love seat and had to be pried apart.

In the meantime, Aunt Lorna was trying to seduce Dennis. She kept running her hands up and down his thigh. "Why can't you boys do it the right way? I think you're the sexiest thing I've seen in thirty years. What do you see in that Billy Lee? He's so young!"

Aunt Clo, who had been sitting in the opposite corner splashing bourbon on herself, stood up and announced, "I think it's time I drive myself home. Yes, I am impaired. But never mind, Jesus will guide me."

I walked her to her car. She stumbled in and push-buttoned the window to a crack. "I think your little friend's just as cute as could be!"

She burned rubber across the lawn.

■

The next evening was dinner at my father's. He barbecued his famous steaks. I met my stepmother for the first time. Little seemed to faze her. She existed in a simple fog.

Toward the end of our supper, I ventured to inquire what might have happened to her fist husband. She pushed a little okra onto her fork and replied, "He blew his brains out in one of them warehouses down by the river. But don't tell my daughter, she thinks he had a coronary. I made a real special peppermint angel food cake for dessert. I sure hope you're gonna like it."

The following morning we left for a trip to the Gulf. My father hugged me goodbye and said he was glad to see me. He referred to Dennis as my "special friend."

■

After a week on our own, we were guests of honor at a dinner party in Houston thrown by my Aunt Carol. I hadn't seen that branch of the family in over a decade. Not a one of them was absent. Even Mother Dear drove down. She appeared wearing a large, strawberry-patterned pantsuit with matching green shoes. She looked more like a clown than I could ever hope to.

Ten conversations occurred simultaneously as we all caught up and no one heard a word anyone said. We drank tumblers of scotch and ate a buffet dinner.

In the center of it all sat a ninety-two year old version of Aunt Killy. Her white hair was coiffed like a queen. She wore a burgundy dress, fashionable heels, and her family pearls. She was confined to a wheelchair for the sake of convenience. When she acted up they simply wheeled her into the guest room and shut the door. Killy had been a tad depressed. Her only remaining son had died that winter. "It's terrible to outlive all your loved ones."

"Now, Killy, don't fuss. You've still got us."

"That is just what I mean."

"You be a good girl and we'll give you something to drink."

"Yeah, fix me a drink. And make it a double!"

My cousin, Betty, who had married one of the richest men in Houston, expounded on the woes of the wealthy. "What I hate is losing ten cents to every dollar my husband brings home all because a bunch of lazy welfare bums would rather collect from the government than work for a living. I'd rather take a welfare family into my own home and put 'em to work myself than lose that dime."

I informed her that slavery had gone out with the Civil War.

I TOOK MY TRUE LOVE SOUTH

"Oh hell, Billy, you've been up in Canada too long. Everybody up there's a communist!"

"I want to die!" screamed Killy.

I went over to tell her hello and that I was sorry about her losing her son.

"Do you think I'm crying for him? I'm crying for Trina! You remember my little dog, don't you? I think about her so much."

"But Trina's been dead fifteen years."

"What is time when dealing with grief? And I'll tell you something, I'll tell you something here and now. I know for a fact she didn't die of no heart attack. Do you see that swimming pool out there? She drowned in one just like it!"

Betty sauntered over and said, "Now Killy, you'd better hush, or we might just see how well you can swim, too."

About two o'clock that morning, those of us with a desire for sobriety went out to that pool for a dip. Those who didn't watched the Royal Wedding on Beta Max. Mother Dear tried to convince Betty that her wedding had been more beautiful than Lady Di's, a feeble attempt to gain confidence.

As we were drying off, my cousin Lynnie confided, "God, look at us. We've know each other our whole lives and we haven't got a thing in common. It'll probably never happen again, but it's been kind of nice being together tonight. We never would have if you hadn't come home, Billy. And especially if you hadn't brought your little boyfriend."

Before I could stop myself, I uttered words I had always dreaded hearing myself speak. "We *are* family."

Out of nowhere, something real ill-like came over me. I fell to the ground and threw up on her feet.

White Woman Turns Black

THE CIRCUMSTANCES SURROUNDING MY AUNT CLO'S death made it difficult to know what form of gesture appropriate. On one hand, it was a blessed relief, as any end to a battle with cancer tends to be. On the other, it was an absurd form of ironic justice.

Clotilde Bedwell was another victim who married into our family. Like Suzy Knocks, she wasn't really one of us. She wasn't even alcoholic. She was worse. The daughter of a Southern Baptist preacher.

More often than not, it was just such a background that bred the most fanatical racists. Of course, Aunt Clo never considered herself so. She probably didn't even know what the word meant. But she had an awful habit of doing things like referring to her more than devoted maid as "that jigaboo out in the kitchen," just to remind her of her place.

The black women then employed by the middle class South cooked, cleaned, and raised the children. While at work, they usually wore white, cotton, starched uniforms. Those uniforms had a particular smell that I always associated with comfort and affection, something I never associated with my mother or aunts.

I will never forget the day Aunt Clo's yardman told her he was schizophrenic. She'd had him for twenty-two years and fired him on the spot. "I can't have a schizophrenic nigra running around my yard! Who knows what he might do, he might try and rape me." She poked at her Adrienne's House of Beauty hairdo, a standard post-bubble with frosted bangs and tastefully tempting spit curls. How well it complemented her collection of classically cut, fortel pantsuits.

For years, Aunt Clo served as Regional President of the Delta Beta Sigma Sorority for young women. She once made national news for a speech she gave on the subject of admitting colored girls into her sisterly bosom.

"Ladies and Gentlemen, every summer at our convention all our young delegates tend to get into the booze. I put up with it to a certain extent, but when a gal goes too far, I've got no choice but to pack her up and send her home. Now, you tell me what'd happen if I had a nigra girl who drank too much and had to be sent home? I'd have the N-double A-C-P on my doorstep before dawn, and I'm not prejudiced. We've just got too many laws about these kinds of things. It's the same way with the E-R-A. We don't need that. This is America!"

Aunt Clo did have another side to her that was a little more endearing. She was the only person I ever knew who was perpetually prepared to forge ahead with practicality regardless of how grand a crisis. Whether orchestrating a wedding, funeral, or divorce, she always did her utmost with a firm sense of what should and should not be done.

When she found out about her cancer, she went through

the first round of chemotherapy and surgery with her usual sense of a job well done. When she was again diagnosed with the disease, she was a little less enthusiastic. The second round left her in pretty bad shape. She was on the verge of not being able to take care of herself, and to someone like Clo, that was worse than any disease could ever be. She was ready to die, but determined to do so alone, and in her own home.

In early February it became clear she would not get any better. Her daughter made the difficult decision that by the end of the month, she would have to be put into a nursing home. Aunt Clo, too weak to argue, made some arrangements and put her affairs in order.

The following weekend, she phoned Mother Dear and asked her if she wouldn't come around for a drink on Sunday. Mother Dear said she'd be happy to. Aunt Clo hung up, went into the bathroom, and shut the door. She spread a quilt out on the floor and lay down. She turned on the small gas heater that was built into the wall, but didn't light it.

The next day, Mother Dear arrived at the appointed hour. She knocked several times, then pushed open the door, finding it unlocked. The smell of gas was, of course, overwhelming. There was a note pinned to a chair nearby. It was so beautifully my aunt. It said, "Sorry to do this to you, dear. Don't come in. Just call Dr. Talbot, he'll know what to do. Please have someone with my daughter when she's told. Enclosed, find your birthday check. My love, Clo."

Mother Dear, not being one to let anybody get away with anything, rushed right in and opened some windows. She began to look for Aunt Clo. Oddly enough, she couldn't find her. Then she noticed the closed bathroom door.

She called the doctor. When he arrived, they opened it together. A very peculiar reaction had taken place between the gas and Clo's body. My mother could not believe her eyes. "Why, she's black! She's turned as black as the Ace of Spades!"

Then the most tragic thing of all occurred, Aunt Clo stirred. Though her body had gone through all the final stages, she wasn't quite dead. They'd found her in the nick of time.

They washed her, scrubbed her, and gave her tea. She died a month and a half later, in agonizing pain, at St. Vincent's Hospital.

Irony, being relentless, was not about to stop there. Aunt Clo was to be buried in the town of Magnolia. Her daughter made the arrangements. The body was to be driven down the morning of the service.

The day before, however, Magnolia elected its first black mayor. A parade and rally followed and the number of black Arkansans present was unprecedented. The roads and small highways within a fifteen mile radius were absolutely clogged. The hearse carrying Aunt Clo was caught in the thick of it and she missed her own funeral.

It was shortly before sundown, and to a resounding chorus of "We Shall Overcome," that the body finally found its grave.

Beyond Happiness

EVERY FEW YEARS I STILL GET THE URGE TO BE IN THE SOUTH. Not Arkansas necessarily, usually I go to the Gulf. I was in New Orleans not long ago. I was working on a new writing project and wanted to be alone.

I woke up one night in the middle of a thunderstorm. I sat at my window and watched the rain bang down on the stone courtyard, the droopy old trees, and the French trellises. I was overcome with the most peculiar urge to see Mother Dear. We'd hardly written or spoken for five years and I just wanted to see her.

I decided I'd rent a car first thing in the morning and be on her doorstep by late afternoon. I sat up the rest of the night flipping through what I'd written. I wanted to throw it away, but didn't.

At dawn, I went around the corner for coffee and biscuits. I was on the road by eight. It was a radiant day, fresh from the rain and very green. That landscape that had always bored me seemed like the most beautiful place in the world. Perhaps it was the thrill of acting on a whim, unharassed, and having the pocket money to pay for it.

When I got to Little Rock, I went directly to my mother's apartment. The superintendent was out clipping the hedge and saw me at her door. He told me she was away. She'd gone up to New York for the long weekend, with a gentleman friend he assumed. Did I want to leave a message? No.

I drove by my father's and found he was away also. I pulled into a gas station. From a phone booth I called Bruce Cocklin. He said he was glad to hear from me and asked if I couldn't stop by.

"No," I said. "I'm short on time. I just called to see how you were."

The next thing I knew, I was walking around the playground of Forest Park Elementary. I thought about how all those kids I used to be so afraid of were now afraid of me. I'd see them, working in the drugstore, behind the checkout counter at the Safeway, or managing one of those franchise restaurants out on the new highway. Then I thought, the new highway. The new highway went straight through Pine Bluff. Why not drive down there? Take a look at the house where we first lived, the street corner where Freddie and I used to watch the rodeo parade line up, maybe even go out to the cemetery.

My father had come from a large family and, except for my grandmother, I'd never known much about them. My mother had seen to that. After all, they were common.

I went out to the cemetery to get their names. The Belle plot was one of the largest on the grounds and covered in ivy. An oak tree shaded most of it. I noticed an old gardener resting on a bench nearby.

I got out of the car and began walking around. I spotted

my grandmother's marker. As I crouched down to read it, I was hit by a rock. The old gardener was throwing them at me. He hollered, "Get out of there, hoodlum!"

"Who, me?"

"It's against the law to mess with a person's grave."

"I'm not messing with anybody's grave. This happens to be my grandmother."

"Who's your grandmother?" He scurried over as best he could.

"She was," I said, pointing. "I'm Billy Lee Belle."

"Billy Lee? I haven't seen you since you was three years old."

"What?"

"I'm Jess, Emmaleen's brother. Last one of my generation left."

"But I thought you lived up North."

"I've come back to die. I work here, grounds supervisor. Kind of like being a outdoor janitor. We've had us a lot of trouble with people defacing the markers. No respect for the living's one thing, but no respect for the dead's unforgivable. You're not living in Pine Bluff, are you?"

"No. Just passing through."

"Interested in cemeteries, I guess?"

"Just this one. I never knew much about this side of the family."

"Well, let me introduce you. This here's my mother. This here's my father. Over there's Aunt Eula. She was wall-eyed. And over there's Aunt Pearl. She married a man twice her junior. Course, I never knew 'em too personal-like. I never had me a wife or any kids of my own so we never did have us too much to talk about. I'm closest to 'em now I water and weed all these graves than I ever was in real life."

"Sounds as though we have a few things in common."

"Most do, though few seem to see that."

When we finished, it was after five. I offered to take him for a whiskey. He was quick to accept and suggested we walk. "What about my car?"

"You can leave it here, ain't nobody gonna hurt it."

Downtown Pine Bluff was pretty boarded up. It was on hold somewhere between the Second World War and the inevitable redevelopment it hoped to soon receive.

We peeked in the windows of the Hotel Pines. It was a landmark, done grandly in Egyptian Deco. It had been owned in its heyday by Jess's father, my great grandfather. My parents had been married there. It was closed in '59.

After several whiskeys in the pool hall, he led me down Laurel Street, not the new part, but the old, where the trees from both sides meet overhead.

"I thought I'd fix you supper," he said.

"Oh that's really nice of you, but I've gotta hit the road."

"It won't take long. I just live up in the next block. It'd be such an honor."

"Okay, but I've got to be gone before dark."

Uncle Jess had the attic room in a run-down boarding house. It was a big place with a porch going around three sides. Old men sat around sadly in sweat stained undershirts talking to themselves.

His room consisted of a cot, an army trunk, a hot plate, a coat rack, a table, and two chairs. The air was sticky and stuffy. I asked him how long he'd been back.

"Seven years. What do you say you and me have us another whiskey?"

He poured them out in juice glasses, then made the motion of a toast. "Hello to happiness." He put it back in one gulp and poured another. "For dinner we got us gizzards. Chicken gizzards on milk toast. They're good for you.

Cheap, too. I eat 'em four to five times a week. Reach over there in that trunk and hand me the bread, will you?"

As I did so, I noticed a name engraved on the side. It was the same name that was on an old army jacket hanging in the corner. "Who's Boy Calder?"

"What?"

"Nothing. I just noticed the name."

"Well you can stop noticing. I didn't bring you up here to meddle, understand?"

"I wasn't meddling."

"That's exactly why I hate people."

We ate dinner in a very awkward silence in which I continually asked myself what I was doing there and why I didn't get up and go.

When he finished eating, he pushed himself back and said, "Do you remember your grandmother had her a black woman, worked for her, lived out back?"

"You mean, Stella? Sure."

"Boy Calder was her brother. He was a friend of mine. We left here together. Nineteen eighteen."

"I see."

"This house you're sitting in. This here's where I grew up. Course, it didn't look much like this then. My daddy had it built for my mama. Boy Calder's just one of the bunch worked for us, until the war. When I come back, I find out all kinds of rumors been passed around about me. Wasn't a very comfortable place to be. Then I find out my father's been the one to start them rumors, all because he was a selfish, manipulative son of a bitch, didn't like the idea anybody might live a little different. I come to think I never should have left Paris."

"Why? You don't mean to say that you and Boy Calder were lov—"

"It's none of your business what we were."

"Well, what happened to him?"

"He was killed, long time ago. Chicago. Ain't much use living if you can't get over things, now is it? But getting over ain't easy when you're old and alone. I'll tell you something. I'll tell you something and you listen to me good. Forget your family. Forget them tombstones and find you something that's alive, 'cause it'll die, soon enough, just like you, and just like me."

I wanted to tell him about Dennis. I looked at the clock and it was almost midnight. I don't even know what had transpired between that old man and I. I don't even know if half of what he'd told me was even true.

When I went to leave, he clutched my hand as though he'd never let go. It seemed so desperate it made me weep. A heavy sadness hung between us, and it wasn't his, it was very clearly mine.

I hated him for keeping me there all night. I had to go through the cemetery in the dark to get back to the rent-a-car.

I drove to New Orleans, went to my room, put together my few belongings, and taxied out to the airport. I phoned Dennis and told him I was on my way home. He said he'd be waiting and that he'd missed me.

■

I hardly remember that flight, but when I got to Canadian Customs I was taken into a room, asked how long I'd been away, and how long I now planned to stay. I answered as though I knew.

On my way home in the taxi, I again looked at what I'd been writing. I read things I knew had happened to me, but had no immediate recollection of, as though somewhere there was a different me, quite separate from who was sitting there.

I walked into my apartment feeling so very odd. In all my attempts to define, dissect, and categorize the South, I had continually failed. In all my efforts to come to terms with the place from which I had come, I had done nothing but grow more alien. There were endless stories and there were endless characters. They were going to be there whether I dug them up and put them on display, or whether I left them there to rot. But somewhere in that garden of haphazard weeds, my part had been penned. It was just that simple. It wasn't a battle, and it needn't be a nightmare.

Exhausted, I walked to my bed. I looked at Dennis's sleeping face and I felt so lucky.

I've had a lot of roles so far. For the most part, I've managed to enjoy them. This mask seems truly mine. And that, Mother Dear, is beyond happiness.

ABOUT THE AUTHOR

Peter McGehee is the author of the short story collection, *The I.Q. Zoo* (Coteau Books, 1991), and the novels, *Sweetheart* and *Boys Like Us* (St. Martin's and HarperCollins). *Beyond Happiness* was originally performed as a one-person play across Canada, in New York, and in San Francisco. Peter wrote the songs for and performed in the musical revues *The Quinlan Sisters* and *The Fabulous Sirs*, both of which toured extensively.

Originally from Arkansas, Peter moved to Canada in the early eighties – to Saskatoon. He died of an AIDS-related illness in September 1991 at his home in Toronto.

ABOUT THE ILLUSTRATOR

Dik Campbell was born in St. John's, Newfoundland and now lives in Saskatoon. His most recent exhibition was *Pressing* about media misrepresentation of gays. Dik is the Production Manager and Art Director of *NeWest Review* and Program Co-ordinator at AKA Gallery.